BABAR
and the Runaway Egg

Abrams Books for Young Readers
New York

One beautiful spring day, Babar and his children took a walk through the countryside.

"Spring is my favorite time of the year," Babar told them. "Look at the new leaves on the trees."

"They're such a pretty green color," said Flora.

"And look at these new flowers," said Babar. "They are daffodils."

"That bird is sitting on a nest!" Isabelle said.

"Yes, that is a mother bird keeping her eggs warm," said Babar. "Maybe they'll hatch soon."

"Uh-oh," said Isabelle. "Look! That egg is getting away!"

Sure enough, one of the eggs had jumped out of the nest and was running down the hill.

"Runaway egg!" Pom cried.

The mother bird jumped off her nest and began chasing the egg, and Babar and the children joined in behind her.

Up hill and down dale they went. They chased the egg past the art museum. "Catch it!" Babar called to the elephants who were nearby. But the egg was too fast for them.

They ran past the playground, but the egg did not slow down.

They ran past the palace, but the egg did not slow down.

Finally, the egg came to a stop all by itself.

"Listen!" said Flora. "What's that sound?"
"Tap-tap-tap. Crack!" went the egg. "Cra-a-ck. Cra-a-a-ck!"

A tiny head popped out of the egg. And then a little bird jumped out.

"Hello, little bird!" said Alexander.

The baby bird hopped over to its mother.

"Peep!" said the little bird.

"Squawk!" said its mother.

The mother and her runaway baby went back to the nest.
"Good-bye, little bird!" said the children.

"Spring is *my* favorite time of the year, too," said Isabelle. "It's full of adventures!"

BABAR
A Gift for Mother

Abrams Books for Young Readers
New York

Celeste's children were excited because Mother's Day was coming.
At school, Pom made his mother a bowl out of clay.

Flora had saved her chore money for months. She bought
Celeste a tiny glass horse.

Alexander chose a shiny silver balloon for his mother.

Isabelle had no present to give. She was too young to go to school and make something, and too little to do chores for money to buy a gift.

She decided to go talk to her father. Maybe he could help. She found Babar in his study.

"Come in!" he said, looking up from his work. Then he saw her face. "Isabelle, what's the matter?" he asked.

"Everybody has a present for Mother but me!" she said.

"Hmmm," said Babar. "Let's think about this. If you could give your mother anything, what would you give her?"

Isabelle remembered what her brothers and sister had done.
    "I would give her a huge bowl made of gold," said Isabelle. "And silver, too. And diamonds."

"Very nice," said Babar. "And what else?"

"And a horse," said Isabelle. "A big pink one. And the bowl and the horse would be delivered by me, in a great big hot-air balloon."

"That sounds like a splendid Mother's Day present," said Babar.

"But I can't give her those things," said Isabelle sadly. "I'm too little."

"You're not too little for a lot of things," said Babar. "Maybe you could find a way to show your mother that you were thinking about her."

"I know!" cried Isabelle. "I can make her a picture! That's something I'm good at!"

Babar smiled. "Let's get out the crayons," he said.

Isabelle drew, and drew, and drew, and drew some more. She filled up the whole paper with color.

And when she was done . . . Ta-da!

On Mother's Day, the family came together to celebrate.
First Pom gave Celeste the bowl he had made.
"What a magnificent bowl!" said Celeste. "I can see you worked very hard on it!"
"I did," said Pom.

Then Flora gave her the glass horse.

"How lovely!" said Celeste. "You must have saved your money for a long time."

"I did," said Flora.

Alexander gave her the shiny balloon.
"What a wonderful balloon!" said Celeste.
"You must have chosen it very carefully."
"I did," said Alexander.

Finally, it was Isabelle's turn.
Celeste untied the ribbon and
unrolled Isabelle's gift.

"Why, Isabelle, what a wonderful present!" said her mother.
"It's a gold and silver bowl and a pink horse," said Isabelle. "And there's me, bringing them to you in a hot-air balloon."
"It's marvelous," said Celeste. "I can see you thought about this gift a great deal!"

"I did," said Isabelle, beaming.

"Do you know what I think?" said Celeste. "I think
I am the luckiest mother in the world!"

BABAR
and the Scary Day

Abrams Books for Young Readers
New York

One day, Isabelle was in Babar's studio, drawing pictures. All of a sudden she heard a noise.

It was coming from above—from the attic. THUMP! it went. THUMP! THUMP!

Isabelle ran next door to the children's bedroom.

"Pom! Pom!" she yelled. "There's a scary monster in the attic! It's green, and it's huge!"

"Isabelle, stop imagining things," said Pom. "There's no monster in the attic."

But just then, there was another loud noise. THUMP-drag, it went. THUMP-drag.

"Eeeek!" screamed Pom and Isabelle.

The two of them ran down the hall to the playroom.

"Flora!" Isabelle yelled. "There's a monster in the attic! It's green, and it's huge!"

"It's dragging one foot!" added Pom.

"Don't be silly," said Flora. "There's no such thing as a huge, green, foot-dragging monster."

Just then, another noise came from the attic staircase down the hall. THUMP-drag-rattle, it went. THUMP-drag-rattle.

"Eeeek!" screamed Pom, Isabelle, and Flora.

The three of them ran down the stairs at the other end of the hall to the kitchen, where Alexander was having a snack.

"Alexander!" yelled Isabelle. "There's a monster coming to get us! It's green, and it's huge!"

"And it's dragging one foot!" said Pom.

"And it's rattling chains!" said Flora.

"Wait a second," said Alexander. "There's no such thing as a huge, green, foot-dragging, chain-rattling monster."

But just then, a noise came down the stairs toward the kitchen. THUMP-drag-rattle-clank, it went. THUMP-drag-rattle-clank.

"Eeeeeeek!" screamed Isabelle, Pom, Flora, and Alexander.

The four of them scrambled into the pantry. They huddled against the door, listening. THUMP-drag-rattle-clank, went the noise from upstairs. THUMP-drag-rattle-clank.

"I definitely think I saw it," whispered Alexander. "It's green. And it had a big bunch of dungeon keys it was clanking."

"What if it comes down here?" asked Flora.

After a few minutes, they realized that the noise had stopped.

"Do you think it's gone?" asked Isabelle.

"Don't know," said Pom, with a shudder.

A few more minutes went by. Finally, they decided to open the pantry door, very carefully.

Nobody was in the kitchen. The house was quiet.

"Look!" said Isabelle, pointing out the window.

Out in front of the palace was Babar. He was piling tied-up bundles of newspapers and magazines, bags of cans, and boxes of bottles at the curb.

THUMP, went the newspapers as he dropped them on the ground. Drag, went the bundles of magazines as he moved them onto the pile. Rattle, went the bags of cans. Clank, went the bottles.

"It's recycling day!" Babar announced to the children. "Zephir and I just went through the whole palace, collecting things for recycling. Whew—it's a monster of a job!"

"We know!" said Isabelle, Pom, Flora, and Alexander.

BABAR
and the
Christmas House

Abrams Books for Young Readers
New York

It was the middle of December, and Babar's four children were excited. They could almost smell Christmas in the air.

Every day Pom, Flora, and Alexander, the oldest children, would walk to school and look at the decorations that had been put up on the houses.

Some of the houses had
beautiful wreaths on their doors.

Some houses had candles in their
windows. They glowed warmly and
invitingly at all who passed by.

But there was one house, way at the top of the biggest hill, that was different. This house had lots and lots of decorations on it.

The children didn't know who lived there. They had heard that someone new had moved in, but they had never seen these neighbors.

Each day it seemed that there was something new to look at. One day, a fantastic structure made of blinking lights appeared on the roof. It went up, up, up, almost to the sky.

Another day, it was an enormous sleigh with reindeer, perched right on top of the garage. The reindeer appeared to be made out of fruits and vegetables. Or maybe it was wood and cloth. It was hard to say.

Every day the children would go home and report to their parents on the progress of the incredible house.

"You have to go and see it!" Flora told Babar and Celeste. "You'll be amazed!"

"We will certainly have to go and see it soon," said Celeste.

Babar looked in his *Big Book of Celesteville Residents*. "Hmmm," he said. "Someone new lives there. We haven't met them yet."

A week before Christmas, a fountain appeared in the front yard of the amazing house. The water jetted up as high as the house, and little fishes played in the bubbles. Colored lights made the water look like a wonderful rainbow.

"I wonder who lives here," said Alexander.

The next day, Babar received a letter. It was from Rataxes, who was king of neighboring Rhino City. The elephants and the rhinos did not get along, so Babar was reluctant to open it.

"What does it say, my dear?" asked Celeste.

"Nothing good, I imagine," said Babar.

Dear King Babar,
   That house on the top
of the hill in your kingdom
is an eyesore. It is ruining
the view of the residents of
Rhino City. A Committee
for Ugliness Removal (CUR)
has been formed, and if
you do not deal with this
problem, the Committee will.

King Rataxes

"Oh, dear," said Celeste.
"I suppose we'll have to go
up there soon," said Babar.

The next day, zillions of colored feathers had been added
to the house. The school had a field trip just to see it.

The following day, sparkly things had appeared, as well
as a large climbing tower festooned with colored lights.

"You must come and see the Christmas house!" said Pom, Flora, and Alexander.

And so, Babar and Celeste walked up to the top of the hill to see what all the fuss was about. Cornelius came too, and so did Isabelle, who was still too little for school.

"Well," said Babar. "This certainly is something."

"It certainly is something," said Celeste.

Just then, along came Rataxes and a number of other rhinos. "A-ha!" said Rataxes.

"A-ha!" said the head of the CUR. "Are you going to do something about this?"

"Hmmm," said Babar.

Then the door of the house opened. Out came an elephant.
Another elephant was behind him.
  "Hello," said the elephant.
  "Hello," said Babar and Celeste.
The rhinos just scowled.

"I am Babar," said Babar. "This is Celeste. Welcome to Celesteville."

"How do you do?" said the elephant, bowing. "I am Hector, and this is my wife, Hortense. We are very happy to be here. We have moved here from the other side of the mountains."

Rataxes stepped forward. "Explain yourself!" he said.
Hector looked puzzled. "What would you like me to explain?" he asked.
"This . . . house!" said Rataxes.

Meanwhile, the children were playing in the fountain, tickling each other with the feathers, and climbing on the tower.

"Ohh," said Hector. "The house. Well, you see, I am an artist, and this house is my Christmas gift to all of you."

"Aahh," said Babar. "So this is *art*."

"Of course," Hector replied.

"In that case," said Babar, "we thank you very kindly."

The rhinos frowned. They did not seem to know what to say. "Well," said Rataxes finally, "if it's art . . ."

". . . I suppose there's nothing we can do about it," said the head of the CUR.

"But we don't like it," said another member. And then they left.

The next day, the trees in front of the house were covered with balloons of many colors.

All of Celesteville came and sang carols in the front yard, while the children batted the balloons back and forth. And when they were done, Hector brought out cider for everyone.

Designers: Vivian Cheng and Chad W. Beckerman
Production Manager: Kaija Markoe

Library of Congress Cataloging-in-Publication Data
for this volume has been applied for.
ISBN 13: 978-0-8109-9308-2
ISBN 10: 0-8109-9308-2

Cataloging-in-Publication Data for the books in this volume
is on file with the Library of Congress.
Babar and the Runaway Egg: ISBN 0-8109-4838-9
Babar: A Gift for Mother: ISBN 0-8109-4837-0
Babar and the Scary Day: ISBN 0-8109-5019-7
Babar and the Christmas House: ISBN 0-8109-4583-5

Printed and bound in China
10 9 8 7 6 5 4 3 2 1

harry n. abrams, inc.
a subsidiary of La Martinière Groupe
115 West 18th Street
New York, NY 10011
www.hnabooks.com